MOLE'S CHRISTMAS WELCOME

FROM "THE WIND IN THE WILLOWS"

Mole and Rat were going home after a long day's hunting with Otter.

They were plodding silently through the snow, when suddenly Mole stopped dead in his tracks. His nose began to quiver with excitement at a certain smell. Then he knew what it was.

Home! His old home, where he lived before he met Rat.

"Ratty!" called Mole joyfully. "Come back! It's my home, my old home! I've just smelled it close by here, really quite close. And I must go to it. I must, I must!"

Rat was too far away to hear Mole clearly. "Mole, we mustn't stop now," he called back. "It's late, and it looks as if it will snow again, and I'm not sure of the way! Come on." And he carried on walking without waiting for Mole to answer.

Poor Mole stood alone on the path and felt his heart was breaking. A big sob gathered deep down inside of him. But never for a moment did he think of leaving Rat. The smells from his old home begged him to come back, but he turned his head away and followed on after Rat.

After some time, Rat stopped and said kindly, "Mole, my friend, you seem very tired. Let's sit down here for a minute."

Mole sank forlornly on a tree stump. The sob he had fought with for so long rose up and forced its way out — and then another and another, until the tears were rolling down his face. Rat was surprised and dismayed to see Mole cry. "What is it, old fellow?" he asked quietly. "What's the matter?"

In between sobs, Mole said, "I know it's a shabby little place — not like your cozy house at River Bank — but it was my own little home. And I went away and forgot all about it. And then suddenly I smelled it. And I wanted it! And when you wouldn't turn back, Ratty — and I had to leave it — I thought my heart would break. Oh dear, oh dear!"

Rat patted Mole gently on the shoulder. He waited until Mole's sobs had stopped and then he said, "Well, now, we'd better go and find that home of yours." And he set off back the way they had come.

"Oh, come back, Ratty, do!" cried Mole, hurrying after him. "It's too dark and the snow's coming! What about your supper?"

"Hang supper!" said Rat. Taking Mole's arm, he marched him back to the path where his friend had first smelled his home.

Mole stood for a moment and then his uplifted nose began to twitch. He crossed a ditch, went through a hedge, over a field and down a tunnel with Rat following right behind.

At last they came to the end of the tunnel. They crawled out and stood up straight. Mole lit a match, and by its light they saw they were standing in the yard by Mole's little front door, with "Mole End" painted over the doorbell.

Mole smiled at the sight of his little old house. He hurried Rat through the door, lit a lamp and looked around. There was a thick layer of dust covering everything. The empty house looked cheerless and deserted. Mole collapsed on a chair and buried his nose in his paws.

"Oh, Ratty!" he cried. "Why did I bring you to this poor, cold little place when you might have been at River Bank by a blazing fire?"

But Rat took no notice. He was running here and there inspecting rooms and cupboards, and lighting candles and lamps. "What an excellent little house this is! So neat! So well planned! We'll make a jolly night of it, you'll see! The first thing we need is a good fire. I'll see to that. You get a duster, Mole, and try to clean things up a bit."

Mole began to dust and polish, and Rat soon had a cheerful blaze roaring in the fireplace.

"Now come with me and let's see what we can find for supper," said Rat. After hunting through every cupboard and drawer they found a can of beans, a box of biscuits — nearly full — a sausage and four bottles of cider.

"There's a feast for you!" said Rat as he set the table. "I know some animals who'd give their ears to be sitting down to supper with us tonight."

Rat had just started to open the can of beans when they heard the scuffling of small feet outside, and a confused murmur of tiny voices.

"It must be the field mice," said Mole. "They go caroling every year before Christmas. They used to come to Mole End last of all for hot drinks and supper."

"Let's have a look at them!" cried Rat, jumping up and flinging open the door.

There stood eight little mice, sniffing and snickering. Then their shrill little voices rose up, singing one of the carols they had learned from their parents.

When the singers had finished they glanced shyly at each other. "Very well sung!" cried Rat eagerly. "Now come in by the fire and have something hot."

"It's just like old times!" said Mole. Then he suddenly sat down. "Oh, Ratty," he moaned, "we've nothing to give them!"

"Leave it to me," said Rat. "Tell me," he asked the oldest mouse, "are there any stores open at this time of night?"

"Why, certainly. At this time of year our stores stay open all hours."

"Then off you go at once and get me, hmm, now let me see ..." Much muttering followed and a clink of coins passing from paw to paw. The field mouse hurried off with his lantern.

The rest of the mice perched in a row on a bench in front of the blazing fire. Rat heated the cider and soon everyone was sipping the warming drink. The mice told Mole all the local news and about all their families.

At last the field mouse came back from the store, staggering under the weight of a loaded basket.

Mole enjoyed hearing news of his old neighbors as he stood by the fire. Soon supper was ready and he sat at the head of the table, watching his little friends' beaming faces.

After they had eaten their fill the mice scurried off, showering Christmas wishes as they went. Their pockets were stuffed with treats for their little brothers and sisters at home.

Rat gave an enormous yawn and said, "Mole, I'm ready to drop. I'll take this bed here. What a fine little house this is! Everything so handy!"

He climbed into his bed, rolled himself in the blankets and fell fast asleep. Mole was tired, too, but before he shut his eyes he looked at his old room. All the old familiar and friendly things glowed in the firelight.

Though he had no wish to change his new life, he was very happy he had come back to his old little home. And as he drifted off to sleep, he thought about the splendid Christmas welcome it had given him.

The characters in **Mole's Christmas Welcome** are classic figures in English children's literature. Mole and Rat are perennial favorites created by Kenneth Grahame in his *The Wind in the Willows*, published in 1908. Kenneth Grahame was born in Edinburgh in 1859. While pursuing a career in the Bank of England, he also contributed to journals and published collections of his stories and essays. A.A. Milne, another creator of children's classics, adapted *The Wind in the Willows* for the stage as *Toad of Toad Hall* in 1930.